THE NINE LIVES OF ADVENTURECAT

by SUSAN CLYMER
illustrated by STELLA ORMAI

A
LITTLE APPLE
PAPERBACK

SCHOLASTIC INC.

New York Toronto London Auckland Sydney

ISBN 0-590-47149-X

Text copyright © 1994 by Susan Clymer.
Illustrations copyright © 1994 by Scholastic Inc.
All rights reserved. Published by Scholastic Inc.
APPLE PAPERBACKS is a registered trademark of Scholastic Inc.

12 11 10 9 8 7 6 5 4 3 2 1   4 5 6 7 8 9/9

Printed in the U.S.A.   40

First Scholastic printing, February 1994

To my beloved daughter,
Micaya Vance Clymer,
who loves animals . . .
and adventures . . .
and a good story.

LIFE #1

"Farewell, farewell
Warm mother's nest!"

From *A Kitten's Melody*

"Children," Mom said to my sister, my two brothers, and me. We sat lined up on the porch step in front of her. Mom stretched. "I've taught you the important skills in life." She arched her back. "I've taught you to climb trees and stalk birds. I've taught you to eat only the tasty bottoms of mice." Mom licked us each on the head. It was the purrrrrrrrrfect motherly lick. "I love you very much."

MomCat held up her sharpest claw.

"Now, it's time for you to live on your own."

She hissed softly and swiped at *me*. Yikes! I tumbled off the step in a backward somersault. MomCat nipped my brother. My sister and my brothers and I dashed away. We huddled under the hedge. "Mom," we cried. *"MeeeeeOOOO-OOOwwwwwMMMMM."*

For two stormy nights, we tried to sneak back into our warm home under the porch of the old farmhouse. MomCat chased us away every time.

With that loving good-bye, my sister and my brothers and I set out to find our own way in the world. My smart sister decided to live in the chicken coop to be near Mom. Purry Brother headed for the barn next door. That left only Brave Brother and me. I had always been the adventurous one. We crouched together under an old car and couldn't find anything to eat except dry crunchy ants.

The next morning a truck turned into

the driveway. I made up my mind faster than a cat can swish her tail. I scurried up the nearest tree . . . in a very wobbly way. I'd never climbed so high. Then I closed both eyes and leaped wildly for the truck. *"Meeeeooowwwww!"* I cried as I sailed through the air. *"Oof!"* I landed in a box of corn. I could hear my brother mewing, but I figured it was each kitten for herself now.

I peered over the edge of the box. A long hairless tail wiggled by in the truckbed. What luck! I chased that mouse around the boxes in the truck. Then I tripped over my paws and bumped my head. The sneaky mouse squeezed out the tailgate! My breakfast had vanished. *Humppphhhh.* I scrambled back up into the box and tried to chew on a piece of corn.

Suddenly, the truck roared . . . ROARED. The fur all over my body stood up. I'd never been so rattled in my life! The truck bounced until I figured my whiskers would fall out. "Good-bye, Mom," I meowed.

"Good-bye, Brave Brother. Good-bye, Smart Sister. Good-bye, Purry Brother." I watched the farmhouse disappear.

Dust from the road flew into the truck. I curled up into a ball and covered my mouth and nose with my stubby tail the way Mom had taught me. Then I fell asleep and dreamed of catching juicy mice.

LIFE #2

"Never consort with humans!"

MomCat's First Rule

I awakened to a hand grabbing me — a *giant* hand that was bigger than all of me. Mom had warned me about humans. I'd *never* seen one this close.

The human lifted me near her face. She had *big* teeth. "Hey, look what was in my truck."

I was sure the human was going to eat me. *"Pffssst!"* I spit. Then I did the only reasonable thing a kitty could do.

I chomped one of those fingers.

"Let go, you little monster!" the young woman shrieked and shook me off her hand.

I flew head over heels through the air and landed under a bush.

What a way to wake up. I crouched, afraid that the human would chase me, but she didn't. She stood by the back of the truck, sucking on her finger.

I was so hungry, I felt dizzy. I was thirstier than after I'd eaten ants. My beautiful fur looked brown with dust. I was in a louder, dirtier place than I'd ever imagined. *"MeeeOOOOOwwwwMMMM,"* I sang in my desperate voice. Roaring tires rushed by me. *"MeeeeOOOOOOWWWW-WWWWWmmmmmmmm."*

"Oh, go away!" the woman yelled. She tossed a corncob *right* at me. Humans must be even more dangerous than Mom had taught us.

I rowled, and leaped forward into the

road. I barely missed being squashed by a tire. Then the tire grabbed my tail! A car roared over my head.

"Help!" I cried. Something screeched, so loudly that I thought the sky was caving in. I ducked my head and ran as fast as I could. I went around a tree and through long grass. I streaked past bushes and a chipmunk. I leaped over a rock.

In midair, I saw water below me. I landed in the pond with a giant SPLASH!

Even my head went underwater. I'd never been in water before. I breathed in the water and choked. Now I was going to die! But my front paws touched something.

I pulled myself up on a rock, spluttering. My heart slowly stopped pounding. It would take MomCat hours to lick me dry. Then I remembered that Mom was gone. I'd never see her again. My tail hurt. I tried to look, but my tail was still too stubby to see. I hadn't thought of myself as little for weeks. Right now, I'd gladly

stay a baby if I could live with Mom again.

I sat in the sun and licked one paw dry, then another. Mom had always said that cats had nine lives. I'd lost one when that car grabbed my tail, and I'd lost a second when I nearly drowned. Clearly, I only had seven lives to go.

LIFE #3

> "Dogssssss! Dogssssss!
> SCORN them, but watch them."
>
> From *A Kitten's Melody*

I set out again hours later, my sore tail drooping behind me. I tried to catch a grasshopper, but the bug hopped too fast. Then I leaped onto the back of a baby bluejay. The bird flapped those wings in my nose. Its mother swooped down and pecked me on the head. *"OwowowOW!"* I cried.

Maybe I didn't want to be adventurous. All I wanted right now was food in my stomach and a warm place to sleep. I stretched my neck up tall and looked around. There were lots of houses here . . . not just one like there was at the farm. Maybe I could sleep under one of the porches. Mice liked porches, too.

I scooted through a hole in a fence. As I crept across the lawn toward a house, I heard a loud growl.

I froze.

In front of me was the roundest dog I'd ever seen, if it was a dog. It had stiff legs and its ears pointed up. The head was as big as my whole body. The teeth looked terrible.

The creature galloped toward me. I couldn't possibly outrun the creature all the way to the porch. There was only one hope. Dogs couldn't climb trees. That's what Mom had taught me.

I turned and raced for the closest trunk. I dug my claws into the bark and scurried straight upward. The dog grunted.

I didn't stop at the first limb or the second. I just kept on going, my ears back,

my heart pounding . . . until I realized that the branches were skinny. I stopped climbing. The branch I was on wobbled in the wind. Beneath me, that monster leaped up and down. It didn't look so big anymore. I held onto the branch with my claws.

I called that dog every name I could think of: "Oaf. Monster. Round-nose. Ugly square-head."

The dog snorted louder and louder.

A human came out of the house. "Pickles!" he called. "You silly potbellied pig. What's gotten into you?"

A pig? I'd never seen a pig before. "Pickles can't catch ME," I rowled.

The pig answered me with louder and louder squeals. The boy crossed the lawn and grabbed her collar. Pickles lowered her head and dug her stiff legs firmly into the earth. The boy dragged the pig to the house. It took all his strength. "Come on, Pickles. *Please* cooperate!"

I stopped rowling. What now? Here I was, stuck up high in a tree.

Then I noticed a kind of shelter *right* beneath me. I inched my way backward along the limb. I sprang for the roof of the small building and crouched there. My stomach growled.

I peered inside the tree house. It looked warm and dry. There was a pillow in the corner. I jumped inside and curled up on the soft sleeping nest. I took a deep breath and sighed. I, the AdventureCat, had to be even more careful. After all, I now had only six lives left.

LIFE #4

"Mom, I wish you could be here
To see what I've caught tonight."

AdventureCat's Own Ballad

A sound awakened me. Mom had told me I had good listening ears. The sound came again. *Creeeeeaaaak.*

Suddenly, the boy I had seen with the pig came up *through* the bottom of the tree house floor! I nearly leaped at his face. Instead, I arched my back. "I'm fierce . . . *rrrrrr*," I rowled in cat language.

The boy almost fell backward. His eyes grew wide. Good, I thought, a person who was properly afraid of me.

Then the boy crawled closer! "Poor kitty. You're just a baby," he said.

I scurried backward up the pillow to get away from him. *"Hissss!"* The pillow vanished under my back feet as my tail end slipped out the window. I was falling! My front claws caught the side of the tree house, and I hung there by both paws. "Helpppp!" I howled. The ground spun beneath me. I was a *goner*.

The boy stuck his arm out the window. He grabbed the scruff of my neck and lifted me inside. "Don't be scared."

My legs wobbled when he put me down. Cats could sure lose lives fast. I only had five left! Still, I puffed up all my fur to warn him. "Staaaaaay awaaaaay."

The boy giggled. "Your tail is bent."

If there is one thing a cat demands, it's dignity. Besides, I wasn't afraid. I extended my claws and swiped at him.

He leaned away from my paw. "You're *wild*. I've never met a cat who wasn't a pet. Wait until I tell Anna."

"I'm freeeeeeee," I insisted.

The boy fiddled with a string on his cutoffs. He didn't appear to understand my words. Humans must not be very smart. The boy scooted to the ladder. "Mom's calling. See you later, dirty cat."

He was gone. I sat down, then bounced back up. Yikes! My tail still hurt. I turned in a circle, trying to see if it was truly crooked. And what did the boy mean, calling me dirty? I wasn't that dirty! What an odd creature this human boy was. I'd have to watch him . . . like I would a mouse.

I leaped onto the roof of the tree house. Dusk was falling, so it was time to hunt. After all, I come from a long line of great hunters.

I caught *one* moth.

As darkness came, I heard a door slam. The boy crossed the yard to climb the tree house ladder. This time, I'd be waiting. I crouched by the opening. When he stuck his head up, I swiped at him. MomCat would have been proud. I'd caught a human.

"Ouch!" The boy gasped and threw something at me. It hit me in the chest, and I tumbled backward. "Take your old pizza!" the boy yelled. "See if I ever bring you something to eat again."

He disappeared. I stood up, a little dizzy. I sniffed what he'd thrown. Food? I ate the meat part first. After that, I gobbled. I even ate the funny green crunchy things. It was the first real food I'd had since Mom kicked me out.

Then I licked my paws and even cleaned my head. My stomach felt purrrrrrfect. I drifted to sleep, amazed. I'd had no idea that humans could bring food.

LIFE #5

> "Hunting for food is a true cat's most important job."
>
> MomCat's Second Rule

I stretched in the early dawn as Pickles snorted and pushed at the grass and flowers and twigs around my tree with her round stiff nose. "Pimple Pig," I scorned.

Then I remembered last night and the pizza. Maybe I could train the human boy to feed me! I was so excited by the idea that I jumped into a pile of colored sticks and rolled them around the floor. I swiped at a rope dangling from a nail.

The boy finally came outside with a bigger human. I climbed out onto the roof of the tree house where I could be seen, but pretended not to notice them. Mom had taught me that trick.

The boy pointed up at me. He wore a bandage on his cheek. I stretched my neck to look beautiful. Then the humans walked *back* into the house. Hah . . . I wouldn't let them ignore *me!* I rowled.

The boy threw open the front door. "Go bother somebody else!" he called. I meowed louder. Any kitty worth its whiskers can howl for hours. So I kept on howling all day long. Pickles rooted around the entire yard, even the flower garden. By nightfall, my throat hurt. And the boy hadn't returned.

Then I saw him through a high lit-up window in the house. The pig was inside, too, so I decided to be brave and try to shinny backward down the tall tree. I hugged the trunk as tightly as I could. I slipped and skidded all the way down. I trotted across the lawn and scrambled up a tree that was next to the house. Then I sat on the branch nearest the boy's window and "talked."

In no time at all, the boy came to the window. He glared at me and started to go away. But I was the AdventureCat! I leaped wildly for the window. I dug my claws into the screen and held on. Brave Brother would have been proud of me.

My head clunked on the window on the other side of the screen. *"Yeooowwww,"* I yelled.

"Oh, Wildcat," the boy said. "You might fall."

"Feed meeee . . . *ooooooowwwwww!"*

The boy unlatched the screen and slid two round things out on the windowsill. I unhooked three sets of claws from the screen and licked the round things. Yum. My training of this human was already working!

"Silly cat," he said. "You like potato chips? I guess you can't be all bad." He set a line of round things on a table where I could see them. He pushed open the screen slowly. He must be trying to knock me off!

I showed him. I zipped around the edge of the screen until I was inside. I leaped for the table and gobbled up all the round things he called potato chips. When they were gone, I stuck my head in his glass and lapped his milk.

Then I looked up and panicked. I was inside a human's nest! I pulled my ears back against my head. The boy must have understood. "Scratch me again, Wildcat, and I will put you in a cage and send you to the Pound."

The cage sounded terrible. The boy reached one finger toward the top of my head. I know it was undignified, but I let him. He touched me right on the spot where MomCat used to lick me. I closed my eyes.

I don't know how it happened, but one thing led to another. I ended up stretched out on his chest, purring. He felt like my brothers and sister, all warm and cuddly in the darkness. I fell asleep and dreamed of being a baby . . . of being safe.

> "A wise cat always lands on her feet."
>
> From *Cat Proverbs*

I opened one eye in the morning light and found myself lying on a human! My hair stood out all over my body.

"What in the world?!" a voice yelled from the doorway. The boy sat up, and I tumbled onto the bedspread.

"SHOO, you uncivilized cat!" Mother cried. "Jesse, how could you bring her in here?" Mother waved her hand at me. I hissed and tried to scratch the hand with my claws.

"Wildcat, no," the boy pleaded. But I knew an enemy when I saw one. I stood and arched my back.

Pickles peered around the door. To my horror, she raced stiff-legged into the room. I swished my tail and climbed right up Jesse. He screeched. I climbed up his pajamas and sat on the top of his head.

Pickles leaped for the bed, but her back feet didn't make it. She snapped at the bedspread with her teeth and slid back down. Then she managed to scramble onto the bed, snorting the whole time.

I held on tightly to Jesse's head and swiped at the pig. "Out!" I commanded. I scratched the monster right on her round nose. She let out an ear-shattering squeal.

Mother dragged Pickles squealing and snorting out of the room. That pig made more noise than six fighting cats. Then the boy tossed *me* to the ground. "You dimwitted, ungrateful cat! You hurt my head!"

A much smaller human raced into the

room. She launched herself at me.

"Careful, Anna!" Jesse cried.

The little girl ignored him. "Kitty!" she exclaimed, with a horrible greedy look in her eyes. "Mine."

I ran. I could face that pig, but not this! The little girl grabbed my sore tail. She *squeezed*.

"*Yeoooooowwwww!*" I shrieked. I leaped for the window ledge and pushed open the screen. I rolled out. But I'd pushed too hard. I kept rolling, right off that sill. I fell nose down through the air, then tail down until I managed to get all four feet aiming toward the ground. I passed tree limbs and another window. Oooohhhhh.

"Wildcat!" the boy yelled.

I hit the ground and the whole world went dark. I couldn't breathe. This would teach me to be friendly with humans.

Somehow, I dragged myself under the porch.

I heard the door slam and footsteps racing across the porch. "She's not here!" the boy cried. "She's dead. Anna, I'll never forgive you!"

The little girl wailed.

"If the cat moved, then she's not dead," Mother said. "Though I certainly wish she'd never arrived. She's a vicious, fierce cat."

I didn't mind that description. I *was* rather fierce. Still, I didn't feel so good. Why couldn't I have gone on living with MomCat? Why hadn't I stayed on the farm?

The boy called for me, over and over. I didn't answer. Let him worry about me. I had some thinking to do. Training a human was more dangerous than I'd imagined. I, the AdventureCat, only had four lives left to live.

And I wasn't even grown yet.

LIFE #6

> "Prooowwwwling the night,
> That's the life for me."
>
> AdventureCat's Own Ballad

I left that evening by moonlight.
MomCat had taught me the proper time
for a cat to travel. I squeezed through the
hole in the fence. Then I crossed yard
after yard, determined to find a wild place
to live.

I kept the full moon at my back. I
attacked leaves and pounced on shadows.
I leaped high for a bug. The moonlight
always made me feel frisky. I arched my

back and swiped at a flower. I stalked through high grass.

High grass?

I stopped and looked around me. There wasn't a human house in sight. Ah, but this was a grand place for a kitten! *"Rrro-ooowwwweeeerrrrrrr,"* I sang. I vowed NEVER to think of humans again.

On the far edge of the field, I discovered a rocky hillside. Lucky whiskers, I'd found a cave! "Anybody home?" I crooned. The cave smelled safe. I stalked inside.

What a perfect home! Still, I needed to give the cave my smell to make it really mine. My body hurt from falling, but not too much. I rolled and rolled in the dirt.

Then I crawled outside to sit on the rocky ledge, my new front porch. The moon slowly crossed the sky. Just before dawn, something moved in MY field. I pounced.

A mouse squealed between my paws. I didn't toss it in the air. I just gobbled, bottom first. Mom would have been proud.

I'd caught my first mouse on my very own. I wished my brothers and sister were here to celebrate.

At that moment, I heard a slight sound. I kept hold of my mouse with one paw and looked over my shoulder. A full-grown tomcat sat behind me. He had tufts in his ears and a chunk out of his upper lip. He had a scar above one eye. "The mice herrrrrreeeeeee arrrrrrrree alll mine," he said.

But I was starving!

With one graceful leap, the tomcat swooped up the remains of my mouse in his teeth and batted me on the nose. "Ssseeee youuuuuuu later, Short Stuff."

"*Ow, ow, ow, meeeeeeooooowwwwww, pssssssstttt,*" I moaned.

I huddled in my cave all day, wondering if ugly Scarface would return. That tomcat could rip my fur to shreds. The next evening, I followed the moon back across the fields. My head hung with failure. MomCat would nip my ears if she knew where I was heading. But I was like a cat following catnip.

I scooted through the familiar hole in the fence. The boy's window tempted me . . . like my old nest under the porch. I climbed up the tree and leaped. My claws caught on the screen. Then I rocked out and in . . . out and in. I soon got that screen opening and banging shut. At the right moment, I wrenched one paw free and hooked my claws onto the inside of the screen. The screen banged on my leg. I threw the screen open again and pulled myself inside.

I didn't announce myself. I just scrambled up the bedspread and crawled onto the boy. He was so warm. I butted at his chin with my head.

"Wildcat," he said sleepily. "You came back."

Just for a good meal, I thought. I fell asleep, purring.

LIFE #7

> "Curiousssss, brave kittens,
> Pay attention to your whiskers!"
>
> From *Favorite Cat Songs*

I slowly stretched on Jesse's chest the next morning. Bird sounds filled the room, tasty bird sounds. Yet I had a more tempting idea than hunting. I could explore the human nest while everyone slept.

I leaped off the bed and peered around the door.

I, the AdventureCat, stalked grandly down the hallway. A shadow moved. The skin on my shoulders rippled. I raced down the stairs and around the front room.

I couldn't help myself. I charged over a chair and under a table. I attacked a plant with a flying leap. I somersaulted into the middle of the room, chasing my tail.

Then my whiskers twitched. I stopped rolling. MomCat had always said that I had the best warning whiskers of any of her children. My whiskers twitched again.

On the couch lay a roly-poly lump with pointed ears and sharp two-toed hoofs. Oh no! Pickles!

I puffed myself up. I walked sideways with my legs stiff to look even fiercer. Pickles opened one eye sleepily. "Be-waaaaaarrre," I hissed. "I'll scrattttch you again." The pig snapped her jaws, then grunted. I danced right past the couch and out of the room.

I'd defeated the monster!

This next room smelled like FOOD. Out of the corner of my eye, I saw a flash of gray disappear around the corner. I leaped. That mouse didn't have a chance.

After devouring the tasty bottom, I was

still hungry. All the good scents in here came from up high. I scrambled onto a chair, then sprang to the counter. I made it! Aaahhhh, I was turning into a great jumper.

I stalked until I found a hole in the counter with water dripping. In that hole was a pan that smelled like chicken BIRD. I leaped in and started licking. What a feast!

"That cat's back — in my sink!!!" the mother human screeched from the doorway.

The shrill words flattened my ears. I hunched over the pan, wailing a "Mine, all mine" song in my throat.

Footsteps pounded down the stairs. The boy raced into the kitchen. "Can we keep her, Mom? Please?" Jesse scowled at me. "Wildcat, stop that spitting."

Mother stared at the pig peering around the doorway. "Pickles, how could you let that tiny ball of fur get past you?" The pig's wagging little tail slumped.

More feet galloped into the kitchen. It was the girl, Anna, who had made me fall out the window! Anna stuck her hand over the edge of MY pan. What if she hurt me again? I scratched her with just one claw in cat warning.

"You've done it now," I heard Jesse say over the girl's wail. Mother lunged for the sink. She turned a knob.

"Yeooowwwww!" I screeched. Water

flooded over my ears and dribbled past my whiskers. I sprang from the sink and skidded into the next room. Before I knew it I was right under the pig's belly. Pickles snorted and started to sit on me. I kept running. The pig pushed at my side with her round hard nose, and I went flying. I landed by a window. Curtains hung by the window, so I climbed.

Pickles squealed louder and louder until she sounded like she was screaming.

I spit at them all from the top of the curtains. Mother grabbed something flat on a long stick. "How dare you hurt my baby?!" She boxed my ears. "How dare you climb my new curtains?" I held on with all of my claws, sure that I was truly dying.

"Mama!" Anna cried. "Mouse head!"

Mother hesitated. "A mouse in *my* kitchen?!"

"Wildcat must have caught it," Jesse answered.

"Of couuuuuurrrrrrse I did," I panted.

Mother looked at the mouse and then back up at me. "Perhaps that cat has a small useful side to her."

"PLEASE let me keep her!" Jesse begged.

"Nobody keeeeps meeeee," I muttered, still dripping wet.

Mother sighed. "*If* you can civilize her, Jesse, then we'll see." Mother put down her broom. "*Maybe* she can be yours."

"Wildcat!" Jesse yelled. "Did you hear that? You have a home!"

I didn't understand. Mother had been dangerous for a moment — until she saw the mouse. I shook my ringing head in confusion.

Did humans like mice, too?

LIFE #8

"Count carefully!
Nine lives are all you get!"

MomCat's Third Rule

I soon learned what "civilized" meant. Jesse sprayed me with a water bottle every time I used my claws. So I lived in the tree house. Every morning, I'd come down to the front porch for food. As long as I moved slowly, Pickles didn't chase me. She did try to eat my food, so Jesse fed me on the railing.

I forgot myself one day and rubbed against Mother's ankles after my meal.

"Shoo!" Mother said. I just purred harder. "I don't like cats!" she insisted.

I felt catly and fierce again. More to the point, I felt full. Still, I didn't know what I wanted to do. MomCat had taught me to keep away from humans. Not only could humans be dangerous, but they were un-dignified. Now, I saw *that* for myself. Why, Jesse liked to play in water! And Mother ran around the yard with the pig dancing at her feet.

I sneaked into Jesse's room each night to let him pet me. One dawn, I awakened and thought of Purry Brother. I couldn't remember what Purry Brother had looked like. Had all of his paws been white? Or only three? I paced across the room. I decided I would spend the day stalking birds . . . and thinking about what I should do.

I trotted to the open window and pushed on the screen with one paw. It didn't move. I was trapped inside! I jumped to the bed and pushed on Jesse's chin with my head to wake him up. Then I ran back to the screen, meowing.

"You can't go outside today," Jesse answered, rummaging sleepily in the drawer by his bed. "We're sneaking out to a cat party. The party is called 'The aCATemy Awards.'" He held up a shirt with a letter on it and a tiny cape. "See. You're going as Superman . . . I mean Supercat."

I hid under the bed.

Later, Jesse watched out the window until Mother and Anna pulled away in the car. He tempted me out from under the bed with a piece of chicken. Then he jumped on me and shoved me in a box. It was a horrible trick.

Jesse carried me outside. I bumped and bounced, like when I left the farm in that truck. Jesse carried me forever. I could hear tires whizzing by.

Suddenly, the street sounds stopped. We weren't outdoors anymore. "We're at the shopping mall," Jesse explained.

Next, I smelled cats . . . lots of cats. This was getting worse. "Give me the little fishes," one cat voice said. "I just love humans," another purred. I quivered.

"We're here, Wildcat!" Jesse declared. "This store is called The Cat's Meow."

"Welcome to the First Annual aCATemy Awards," a woman announced. "Did you bring your pussycat, young man?"

Jesse opened my box and lifted me out.

"Good," the woman said. "Be sure and pick up your catnip treat before you leave."

Jesse pulled the little shirt over my head and tied on the cape. I was so rattled that I didn't scratch him like a dignified cat should. I hid my head in his shirt.

After a while, I opened my eyes. I couldn't believe what I saw! One fat gray cat lay draped along a fat man's shoulders. A longhaired white female walked on a *leash* wearing a bonnet with ribbons! Some of the humans even wore furry costumes. Cardboard cats hung from the ceiling.

"Anyone want a kitten?" a girl cried, holding a basket of mewing babies.

Jesse kept talking about the pictures on the walls of cats dressed to look like movie stars. He liked the cat cartoons, too. Jesse chatted with strangers and held me up to show me off. I wished I could disappear. When Jesse leaned over a table of food, I snagged a little fish off a plate to make myself feel better.

"Wildcat!" he exclaimed. Then he laughed. The table was covered with fish-shaped mounds of food. "Tuna." Jesse read the labels and filled his plate. "Salmon mouse." Then he put the whole plate on the ground for me to eat.

Aaaahhhh, if this party meant food, I might survive.

Before I'd finished, Jesse scooped me up.

He dropped me in the middle of three BIG cats. "Look! All of these cats are orange," he said. "Maybe one is your mother."

No such luck. I was surrounded by three unfriendly strangers.

My fur fluffed up in horror. "Hoooowwww could youuuuuu?" I rowled at Jesse. The tomcat hissed back at *me*. Another cat swiped. I yelped and danced sideways. Jesse grabbed my crooked tail. I don't think he meant to, but it was too much.

I ran.

My cape flew out behind me. Jesse yelled. There were so many people, I had to zigzag between feet. A woman lunged for me. One boy almost stepped on my tail. I climbed right up the back of a man who was wearing a furry cat suit. I leaped from his shoulder to the open door.

I was free! I streaked down the hallway. I ran through a double doorway into a small room. The doors closed behind me . . . by themselves! Every hair on my body stood up. The room started to sail

upward. "Heeeelllllp!" I cried. Mom had warned me about magic! This was my end *forever*.

The movement stopped. The doors opened. I sprang out, yowling at the top of my cat lungs. A man gasped and stumbled back. I skidded down a hallway and into a dark room. I hid behind some boxes.

Then I sat and shook.

I chewed on my cape strap. I needed to think. It was important. I had to remember how many lives I'd lost . . .

Life #1 — When the tire grabbed my tail.

Life #2 — When I almost drowned in the pond.

Life #3 — When the pig chased me up the tree.

Life #4 — When I slipped backward out of the tree house.

Life #5 — When I fell from Jesse's second-floor window.

Life #6 — When I met Scarface and nearly starved.

Life #7 — When I was beaten by Jesse's mother with a broom.

Life #8 — When I flew up in a magic room.

I wasn't sure about losing life number six. I was *certain* of the rest. I probably only had this ONE life left. Cats only get nine lives. That's what Mom had taught me.

I cowered in terror, afraid to even move. I crouched in that room for a long, long time. Then I heard a familiar voice, "Here, Wildcat."

Jesse! He would save me. I almost leaped from my hiding place. But that would be undignified. I straightened my tail as much as I could. Then I stalked out. The cape dragged between my front legs.

"Wildcat!" Jesse dropped to his knees

and hugged me. The hug felt good. "I promise I'll never take you to a shopping mall again." He untied the cape. "Ah, poor kitty."

I hate to admit it, but I purred. I was so glad to see Jesse! That's when I made my decision. I didn't care if Jesse was a human. I rubbed my head against his shoulder. I rubbed against his damp, tear-streaked face. If I only had one life left to live, I'd live it with Jesse.

LIFE #9

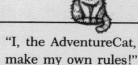

> "I, the AdventureCat,
> make my own rules!"
>
> AdventureCat's Own Ballad

I rode home inside Jesse's shirt, not in that box. When I got there, I moved into the house. No more tree house for me. Jesse's mother sent him right to his room. I shared the turkey sandwich that she gave him.

Then I started planning. Jesse had already proven he was smart enough to find food for me. I had trained him well. Now, I had a new task in front of me, a true cat challenge. I wanted to rule the entire house. I had a feeling that any cat worth her whiskers ruled the house.

MomCat wouldn't approve of my living here, not in nine lives. I was breaking her #1 rule — No consorting with humans. Yet, I knew from my cat claws to the tip of my tail that living with Jesse was right for me.

The next morning, I started my campaign by bringing Jesse's mother a mouse — a whole mouse. I laid the offering carefully in front of her feet. She gasped. Then she said, "Good kitty," in a strangled voice. I leaped onto her lap and purred.

Next, I began sleeping close to Pickles. Each afternoon, I hunched near her in the sunshine and pretended to be asleep. Then I sidled a bit closer to her feet. Pickles snorted under her breath nervously. "Aren't Pickles and Wildcat cute?" Mother exclaimed.

All I needed from Anna was to be left alone. I took to swiping at her toes when she walked by Jesse's bedroom door.

I slept with Jesse every night. I purred extra loudly whenever he brought me chicken legs or pizza from dinner. Before he went to sleep, Jesse always dangled string off the side of the bed. It looked like a mouse's tail. I pounced in wild fierce leaps. Then I sprang onto Jesse's chest, and he stroked me right between my eyes. That boy felt as special to me as my brothers and sister, even if he didn't have fur.

I did my job well. I prowled the house from top to bottom every day, holding my tail so proudly. I was big enough to see its crooked tip now. I learned every mouse-hole and window ledge. I rid the house of every bug. I cleaned myself until my fur shone, so that I looked like a proper ruler.

One morning, I almost ruined my whole plan. Mother was sitting on the couch talking on the phone. From behind I could see her frizzy hair bouncing up and down as she talked and laughed. The hair looked alive. I lost control. With a "Here I come!" rowl, I sailed onto her head. She screamed so loudly that I was suddenly afraid she might make me live outside again. I spent hours finding her a mouse.

When winter drew near, I discovered Pickles's warmth. Every morning when Jesse left for that place called school, I would creep up onto the pig's back and curl up in a ball to sleep. My new friend's grunts quickly changed to soft snores.

Each afternoon, I waited for Jesse to come home. I met him at the front door. So did Pickles. I wrapped myself around his legs. I led him into the kitchen and shared his after-school snack. Then I carried off his colored sticks in my mouth or lay on his papers while he tried to draw.

At times like that, I often thought about my early life under the farmhouse porch.

I hoped Brave Brother and Smart Sister and Purry Brother had done well, too. What a life I had made for myself!

I, the AdventureCat, owned a human now.

ABOUT THE AUTHOR

Susan Clymer likes animals. She likes to walk in the wilderness and do things that seem impossible. "But most of all," she says, "I love to write."

This is the fifth book that Ms. Clymer has written for young readers. Her other books are *The One and Only Bunbun, The Glass Mermaid, Four Month Friend,* and *Scrawny, the Classroom Duck.*

When she's not busy writing her own books, Ms. Clymer visits schools, reads to children, and helps them write stories, too.

She has a daughter, Micaya, and lives in Fairway, Kansas.